Date Due

FANCY BE GOOD

FANCY BE GOOD

WRITTEN AND ILLUSTRATED BY

Audrey Chalmers

jc353p

NEW YORK · THE VIKING PRESS · 1941

First Published September 1941
Second Printing August 1942

TO JO

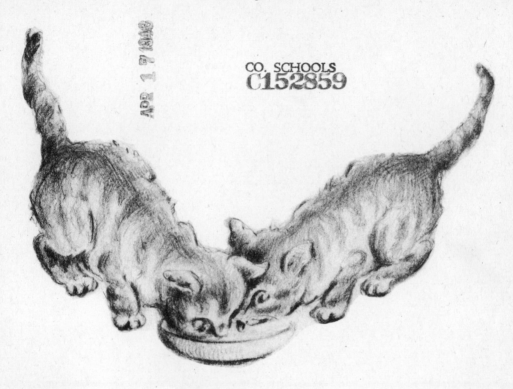

Fancy was a kitten.
So was Mercy.

Every night they slept on the foot of Lydia's bed instead of in their own basket. They looked exactly the same. But they were different. Their manners were different.

One morning Lydia thought: "Oh, dear me! I must remind Fancy not to spill milk on the clean kitchen floor." So she did. But Fancy paid NO attention

and Bedelia did not like this one bit.

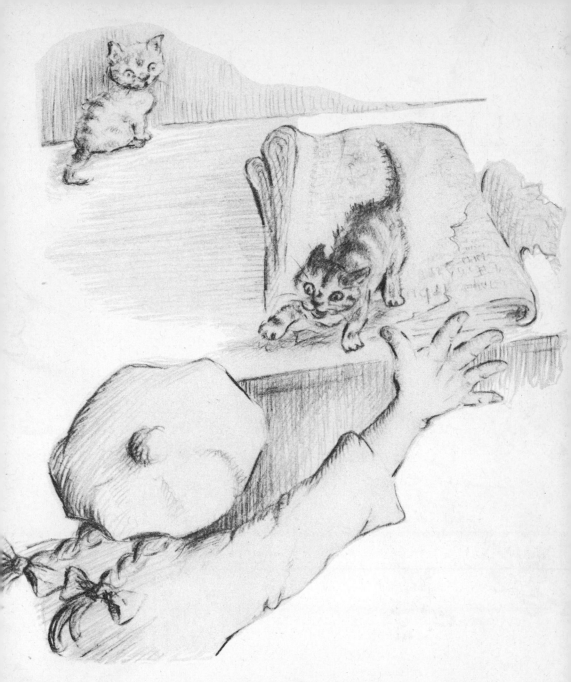

Then Lydia thought: "Oh, dear me! I must remind Fancy not to tear up the morning newspaper." So she did. But Fancy paid NO attention

and Mr. Brown did not like this one bit.

Then she reminded Fancy not to scratch the upholstery.

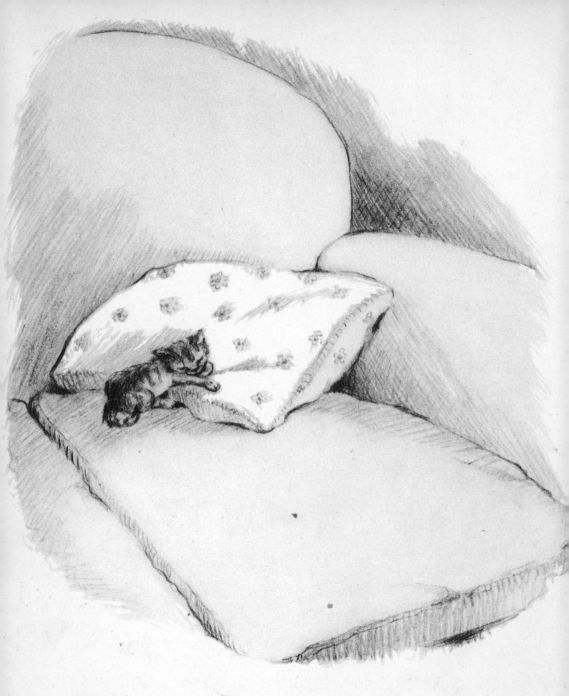

And not to go to sleep with her head on Mother's best pillow.

And not to practice climbing up trees on the Company's skirts. But Fancy did not pay ANY attention to ANY-THING!

So then Lydia reminded Fancy most particularly not to go after the Birds in her Father's garden.

And still FANCY DID NOT PAY ATTENTION! The
Gardener saw it! He went right off to tell Mr. Brown.

Mr. Brown was very angry. He called everyone into the
living room. "I have made up my mind about this
naughty kitten," he said firmly. "She must go away.
She must go to live in Farmer Jones's barn down the
road."

"Oh, Fancy," sobbed Lydia, "why didn't you pay attention!"

Away went Fancy in the market basket. "Mee-yow!" she cried, trying to get out. "No, you don't!" replied the Gardener. On he went.

Pretty soon they came to Farmer Jones's barn. A fierce-looking cow stared out of the door. "Mee-YOW!" cried Fancy again. "Oh, no, you DON'T!" replied the Gardener. He put Fancy down on the barn floor and left.

"Mee-yow?" asked Fancy, looking round. The Horse gave a horrid laugh. "Moo-moo!" grunted the Cow. The Hen looked down her bill, while the Dog gave a short bark and walked off.

After a while Fancy began to practice climbing trees up the Cow's leg.

SLAM BANG! The Cow kicked Fancy over against the wall. "Perhaps that will teach you a lesson!" she said.

By and by Fancy began to practice catching birds on a yellow chick. "Peep!" cried the Chick. "Mumma! PEEP!" "Cluck! Cluck!" answered the Hen. "Mumma's coming!"

The Mother Hen flew at Fancy. "Perhaps THAT will teach you a lesson!" she cackled.

Then Fancy felt tired. So she curled up on the Dog's bed and went to sleep. Back came the Dog. "Whose bed do you think this is?" he snarled.

He shook Fancy until she was dizzy. "PERHAPS
THAT will teach you a lesson!"

After that Fancy crept into a corner, and just thought.
She thought about all the things that she must not do. It
took a long, long, long time.

When it grew dark Fancy crept out of the barn.

She walked along in the moonlight. She did not know
where she was going. But she just walked along.

When it grew darker and darker Fancy lay down
where she was, and went to sleep.

In the morning Fancy woke up. The first thing she saw was her own fence. So she walked in through the gate and there was the same garden and the same fence and everything was the same except herself. But now she was so good that everyone thought she was Mercy!

The Gardener thought so. "Sure, the Birds can take their comfort in the garden now," he smiled.

Mr. Brown thought so. "Well, well! I'll be able to read my newspaper all in one piece for a change!" he exclaimed.

Mrs. Brown thought so. "What a blessing not to worry about my best pillow!" she said.

Even Bedelia thought so. "Come in and welcome!" she cried, and she poured out a bowlful of milk for Fancy,

who drank it all up to the last drop.

"Thank goodness I won't be badgered and bothered with spilt milk any more." And Bedelia sat down with the kitten and stroked her along the back.

Down the stairs came Lydia with Mercy. "A barn must be a lonesome place to sleep in poor Fancy," she was thinking. She came to the bottom step. "A barn must be a lonesome placc to drink milk in."

She came to the kitchen. "Prr-rp! It's ME!" purred
Fancy.

Then Fancy ran to Lydia, who picked her up and
Mercy too, one over each shoulder.

"What!" cried all the Family. "Don't tell me that good kitten is Fancy!"

"WHAT!" cried the Gardener. "Don't tell me that good kitten that never bothered the Birds in my garden is FANCY!"

All day long Fancy was so good that by night time she was simply exhausted. And Lydia went to bed one whole hour earlier

so that Fancy could have a good rest on the foot of her bed, where the kittens slept as usual instead of in their own basket.